D1306222

LOUANNE NORRIS & HOWARD E. SMITH, JR.

An Oak Tree Dies and a Journey Begins

ILLUSTRATED BY ALLEN DAVIS

CROWN PUBLISHERS, INC., NEW YORK

10 9 8 7 6 5 4 3 2 1

The text of this book is set in 14 point Fairmont. The illustrations are black-and-white line drawings.

Library of Congress Cataloging in Publication Data
Norris, Louanne, 1930-   An oak tree dies and a journey begins.   Summary: A big, old oak tree on the bank of a river is felled by
weather and age and, after experiencing life on the ground, in the river, and at sea, is claimed from a beach as a lovely example of
driftwood. [1. Driftwood—Fiction. 2. Natural history—Fiction] I. Smith, Howard Everett, Jr., 1927- joint author. II. Davis, Allen.
III. Title.   PZ7.N7925Oak   1979   [E]   79-14061   ISBN 0-517-53723-0

An Oak Tree Dies and a Journey Begins

A big, old oak tree grew on the bank of a river. During the summer its green leaves hid many of its branches. Other branches were dead and bare. Light gray bark covered most of its trunk. Once the oak had had firm, pale brown wood under its bark. But over the years parts of it had rotted and turned gray. The tree had a few large holes in its trunk. And here and there branches had broken off.

One autumn night the biggest storm in years shook the old oak tree. Its yellow and brown leaves quivered. Many of them were whipped away. The tree swayed and creaked. The wind pulled at its roots. The wind blew very hard. Some of the roots that were rotten broke, and the tree fell to the bank.

All winter long the oak tree lay on the bank. Its top branches lay in the river. Ice formed on them. Many twigs broke. The rest of its leaves fell off.

In the spring more rain than usual fell. The water rose. The river flooded and spilled over the bank. The water became so deep that the tree began to move. It floated downstream with the current.

The swift flowing water carried the tree past forests and farms. The tree almost got caught at a bend in the river, but the current moved it along. Branches, bottles, and an empty rowboat bobbed along beside it.

The racing water pushed the tree into the sandy shore of a small island. The water forced the tree's dead roots into the sand, and the roots held. The flood stopped. The water went down, and the tree stayed.

Where the sun shone on the tree, the wet wood dried out. The bark split in many places, and most of it fell off. The wood turned gray, stiff, and hard. Some of the driest parts looked almost chalk white in the sunlight.

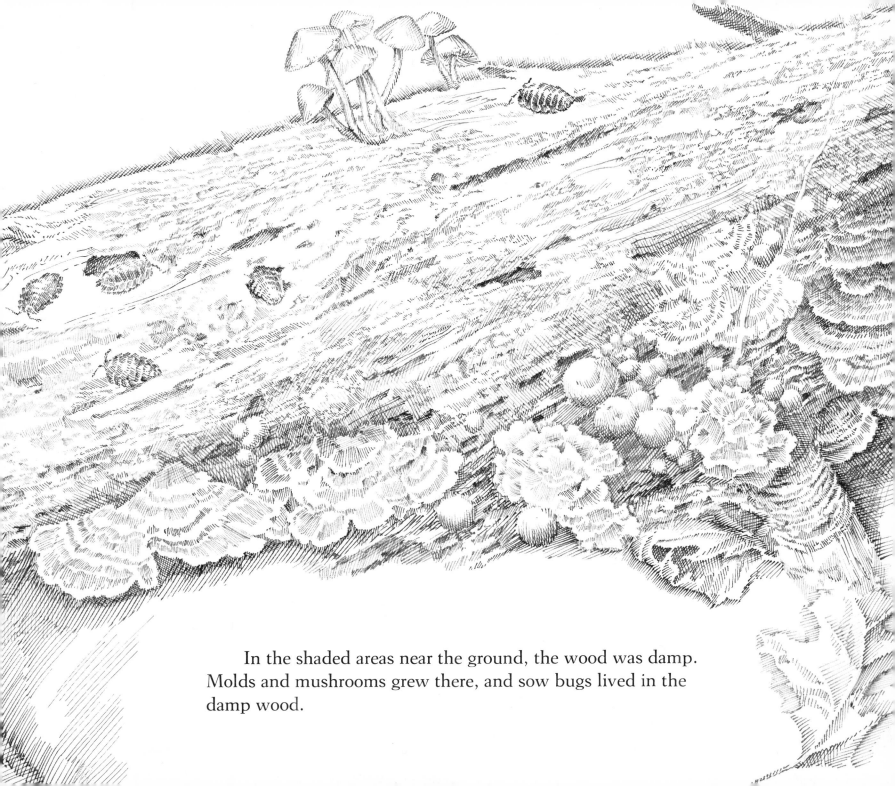

In the shaded areas near the ground, the wood was damp. Molds and mushrooms grew there, and sow bugs lived in the damp wood.

Not all of the tree was on land. Many of its upper branches were under the water. They turned very dark, but they did not rot.

A female raccoon found a hole in the dried-out part of the tree. During the day she slept in the hole. At night she went hunting along the river for frogs, fishes, and small birds. She dipped the food in the river to soften it so that she could easily swallow it. In the winter she mated with a male raccoon. The following spring she had babies.

Frogs swam in the still water near the tree. They hopped up
onto the branches. Their eyes blinked, and they turned their heads.
When black snakes crawled along the trunk of the tree, the frogs
leapt into the water. When dragonflies flew by, the frogs snapped
at them with their long tongues.

Minnows darted under the tree's branches. Yellow perch, pickerel, suckers, and other fish swam nearby. Sometimes big river bass hid in the dark shadows of the tree. When smaller fish swam by, the bass swam out and swallowed them.

Two children often sat on the tree and fished. They knew that bass hid among the branches. From time to time they caught one. The tree lay on the island for a few years.

But one spring heavy rains fell again, and the river flooded. The water got very deep and moved very fast. Soon water covered the island, and the tree floated away.

The tree moved downstream with the current. The river became wider. Other rivers poured into it. The tree passed factories, buildings, and bridges. Ships went by; their waves splashed the tree and rolled it over in the water.

The tree floated out to sea. It moved up and down on the waves. On windy days the waves were so big that the tree would ride to the top of a wave and then glide down the back of it with its roots pointed toward the sky. The waves broke and smashed at the tree and pushed it deep into the water, but it always came up again.

On calm days the tree bobbed gently in the water. Gulls and terns flew over it. Some of the birds landed on the tree and rested. They cleaned their feathers and turned their heads this way and that way as they looked around.

A few weeks later, a bright green seaweed called mermaid's-hair started to grow on the tree. Gooseneck barnacles, mussels, oysters, and other animals with shells attached themselves to the tree. Brown seaweed trailed in the water. Small, dark green fish called cunners and young sea bass swam for hours under the tree. They ate the barnacles, oysters, and mussels, and nibbled on the seaweed.

Seawater soaked into the wood, and the wood became darker and softer. The tree was heavier, and it floated deeper in the ocean waters. Almost all spring and summer the tree drifted in the ocean.

Late in the summer a storm blew up. The wind blew very hard, and the waves became larger and larger. Huge waves crashed on a rocky shore.

For two days and two nights the waves battered the tree against the rocks. More branches and roots snapped off. The wood split; chunks of it fell off and drifted away. The rocks smoothed the wood. Almost all the seaweed, barnacles, and oysters were scraped off. After the storm, the tree no longer looked like a tree. It still had a few roots, but it was a battered log rolling in the water.

The log drifted close to shore. Some girls at a beach climbed onto it, and the log became their boat. They took other pieces of wood and paddled with them. Then they pulled the log out of the water and onto the sand.

A very high tide carried the log farther up the beach. A strong
wind helped push it along. The log became stuck in the sand.

Over the next few months wind blew sand over a part of the
log. Slowly the remaining barnacles dried out and fell off. The log
began to dry out, and grass roots grew over parts of it.

Beetles crawled on the log. They gnawed little tunnels through
the wood. Then they laid their eggs in the tunnels.

A rat built a nest under the log. It lined the nest with twigs
and paper. At night the rat ate grass seeds and hunted on the beach
for dead fish and other food. Then the rat scurried back to its nest.
It poked its nose out, looked around, and popped back in again.

Beachcombers sawed off parts of the driftwood log for firewood. Sparks popped out of the fires. The flames were colored blue, green, and orange by the dry sea salts in the old wood. People enjoyed watching the flames at night.

Part of a root remained on the log. The root was gnarled and bent. For over a year sand blown by the wind had rubbed against it and polished it. In the sunlight it shone silvery gray.

One day a boy found the driftwood on the beach. He broke
off the root and held it up. He liked its twisted shape and its colors,
so he took it home and put it on a shelf in his bedroom. Whenever
he looked at it, he thought of the beach. And sometimes he wondered
where the driftwood had come from and what had happened to it
along the way.